D1509951

398.2
STJ

3 66433 0903995 1
StJohn, Amanda.

Coyote rides the sun
: a Native American
folktale

$19.00

DATE DUE	BORROWER'S NAME	ROOM NO.

398.2
STJ

3 66433 0903995 1
StJohn, Amanda.

Coyote rides the sun
: a Native American
folktale

COYOTE RIDES THE SUN

A NATIVE AMERICAN FOLKTALE

retold by Amanda StJohn • illustrated by Durga Yael Bernhard

Distributed by The Child's World®
1980 Lookout Drive • Mankato, MN 56003-1705
800-599-READ • www.childsworld.com

Acknowledgments
The Child's World®: Mary Berendes, Publishing Director
The Design Lab: Kathleen Petelinsek, Design
Red Line Editorial: Editorial direction

Library of Congress Cataloging-in-Publication Data
StJohn, Amanda, 1982–
    Coyote rides the sun : a Native American folktale / by Amanda StJohn ;
illustrated by Durga Yael Bernhard.
        p. cm.
    ISBN 978-1-60973-138-0 (library reinforced : alk. paper)
    1. Indians of North America—Folklore. 2. Coyote (Legendary character)
I. Bernhard, Durga, ill. II. Title.
    E98.F6S762 2012
    398.2089'97—dc23   2011010892

Printed in the United States of America in Mankato, Minnesota.
July 2011
PA02086

ook, look! In the field . . .
a coyote! Isn't it handsome?
Well, don't let Coyote's good looks fool you.
He's a clever fellow, and curious, too.

Native American desert people, called
the Paiute, have a story about Coyote's fur.
Once, Coyote's fur was the color of desert
sand and that's all. But one day, Coyote
rode on the back of the sun, and his fur
changed forever. . . .

I remember the day Coyote was born. Old Man, the creator of the world, came to visit him. Pokoh—that is Old Man's name—loved Coyote. Pokoh taught him to hunt squirrels and rabbits.

Coyote always wanted to gobble up his food. If Pokoh hunted a rabbit, Coyote ran to eat it. He ran so fast a cloud of desert sand swirled up behind him. Seeing the dust, Pokoh put up his hand like a stop sign. Coyote skidded to a halt.

"Thank Rabbit for his life, first," instructed Pokoh. "Then you may eat."

Woo-wooooooooooo! From that day on, Coyote howled with gratitude before each meal, and Pokoh was pleased.

When he finished eating, Coyote spit on his paws and licked them clean. He sat down to warm himself in the sun. That's how he fell in love with the sun.

Well, one day, Coyote went to Pokoh, who was fishing. "Old Man," he said, "I want to meet the sun. Will you introduce us?"

Pokoh thought on this for a moment. "I can't today," he said. "But I will tell you the way to the ground hole where Sun comes up each morning." So he did.

Coyote bounded toward the sun. He chased Sun but could not catch up with him. Sun went around all day, and Coyote found himself back where he had started.

The next day, Coyote visited Pokoh. "Old Man," he said. "I followed your directions to the hole where Sun comes up, but I arrived too late. Do you know a shortcut?"

Pokoh thought for a moment. "When I was a boy, I took a different route through Tule Marsh."

So Coyote bounded toward Sun's
hole. His long legs paddled through Tule
Marsh. Coyote swam so fast Perch could
not keep up with him.

At last, Coyote saw the hole where
Sun comes up, but he was too late. Sun
was already in the sky. Sun went around
all day, and Coyote could not catch up
with him.

Hahrooo! Coyote cried and cried. But finally his tears were all used up, and Coyote made up his mind to try again.

The next morning, when Sun tried to come up out of his hole, Coyote was in the way.

Sun said, "Hey! Move, you! I have work to do."

"Move, you. I have work to do!" Coyote sang back.

Sun tried to bump Coyote out of the way. Coyote sprang into the air—yip! He landed headfirst inside the hole.

"Move! MOVE!" shouted Sun. "I must rise now!"

"Oh," said Coyote, pretending that he couldn't hear. "What a nice, long night it is!"

"Okay, then," said Sun hopelessly. "What must I do to get you to move?"

Coyote sprang up. "Sun," he yipped, "I want to ride across the sky with you!"

"No way," Sun said, but Coyote wouldn't give up.

"Climb on my back, then," huffed Sun.

Sun began walking across the sky as
if he was climbing stairs. "One, two,
three . . ." he counted on and on.

Sun grew hotter with each step.
Coyote's fur started to smoke. *Haaroooo!*
The tip of Coyote's tail turned black.

At noon, Sun's heat was fierce. Coyote licked his dry chops. "Sun," he said, "I need some water."

So Sun gave Coyote an acorn-cup of water. "Sun," Coyote whimpered, "is that really all the water you have?"

But Sun just kept on counting and climbing. He grew brighter and hotter.

HAAROOOO! Coyote yelped in pain. "Close your eyes and rest," Sun told him.

Coyote closed his eyes and felt better. Once in a while, he would open them to peek at the ground below him.

At last, Sun came to the end of his journey. Coyote was so relieved. He leapt into the first Juniper tree he could reach.

From that day forward, Coyote's
fur looked as if it had been toasted like
a marshmallow. Coyote hid from Sun
during the hot hours of the day. He
closed his eyes and took long naps while
waiting for the earth to cool down.

I asked Coyote once if he'd like
to ride the sun again. "No way!" he
whimpered and scurried away into
the desert.

Canada

Canada

The Southwest

United States

Mexico

FOLKTALES

Imagine you are gathered around a campfire with everyone you know. Here, your elders share wonderful folktales, or stories learned from others. The best storytellers will make you laugh and weep, which helps you remember a story and its lessons. In this way, *Coyote Rides the Sun* was shared amongst the Paiute peoples of North America for hundreds of years.

The Paiute lived in a region of the United States called the Great Basin. This includes Arizona, California, Idaho, Nevada, Oregon, and Utah. Some bands of Paiute live in hot deserts, like Coyote. Others live near lakes or wetlands, such as the Tule Marsh.

A tule (pronounced *TOO-lee*) is a type of plant that grows in wet places. Some Paiute collected young tule sprouts and flowers to feed their families. Tules can also be cooked down to make dye, or woven into basket hats. No wonder Old Man Pokoh has fond memories of the Tule Marsh!

As for Coyote, he is a famous Native American character that appears in hundreds of unique folktales. Coyote stories were cherished by all, so many individuals wanted to contribute a Coyote story of their own. The best of these were remembered and retold by the people.

Sometimes, Coyote is an animal, and sometimes he is a man. In any case, Coyote is usually selfish. He loves to win and hates to lose. Sometimes, Coyote cheats and lies, but this usually backfires on him. Coyote teaches us how to behave by showing us what *not* to do.

23

ABOUT THE ILLUSTRATOR

Durga Yael Bernhard is the illustrator of numerous children's books, with topics ranging from natural science to multicultural themes. She has a deep love of African culture, Eastern and Western religion, and the natural world, all of which are reflected in her art. Durga's experience mothering three children has also shaped some of her most notable works, including *A Ride on Mother's Back: A Day of Baby-Carrying Around the World*. Durga is most known for her innovative concept books such as *In the Fiddle Is a Song: A Lift-the-Flap Book of Hidden Potential* and *While You Are Sleeping: A Lift-the-Flap Book of Time Around the World*.